Filbert
the
Good Little Fiend

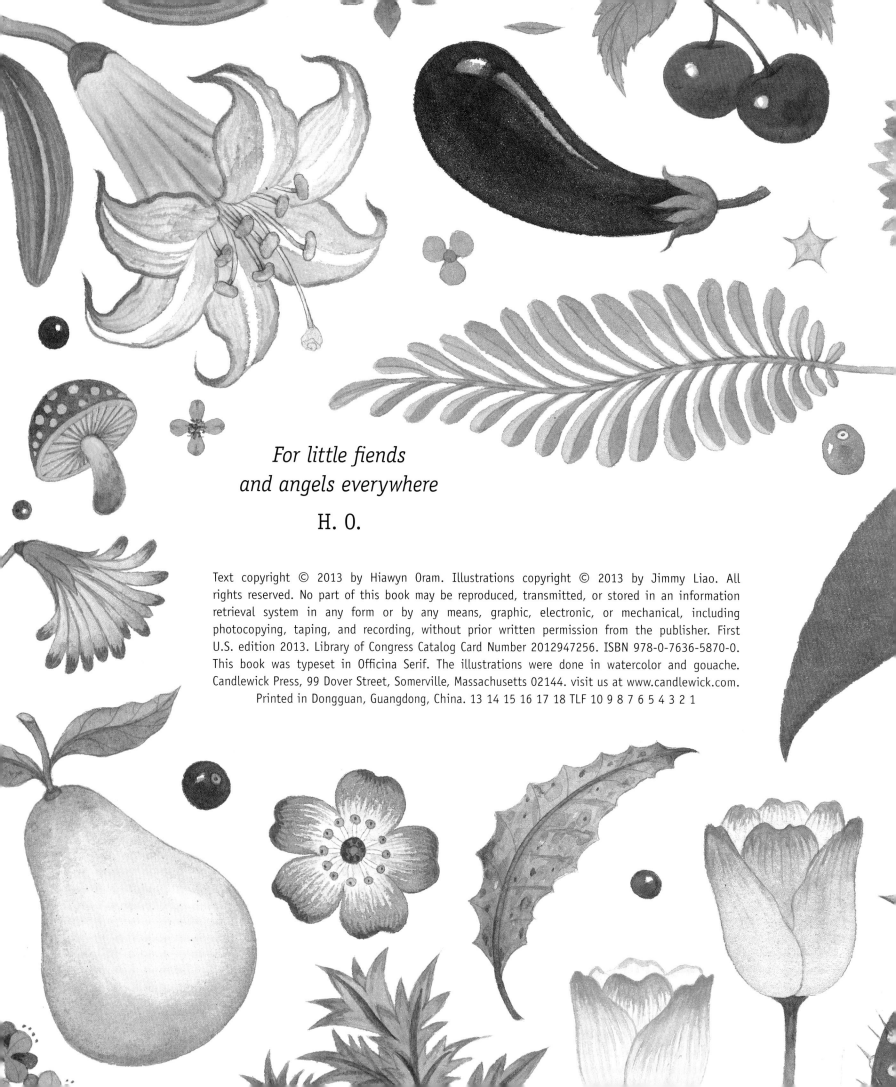

*For little fiends
and angels everywhere*

H. O.

Filbert
the
Good Little Fiend

Hiawyn Oram   Jimmy Liao

CANDLEWICK PRESS

Once there was a
Daddy Fiend, who was
FEROCIOUSLY fiendish.

There was a Mommy Fiend,
who was FIERCELY fiendish.

And there was Filbert,
their little fiend,
who was good,
good, GOOD.

"What's the matter with him?" said Daddy Fiend
fiercely. "He won't say BOO to a goose,
MOO to a moose, or PANTS to an ant.
He's no little fiend of mine!"

"You're right," wailed Mommy Fiend as she helped Filbert
into his fiery red coat, horrifying horns, and monstrous mittens.
"Now," she said, "we're all going out to be gruesome and ghastly —
you, your daddy, and me."

But Filbert wouldn't be
those things. He wouldn't HUFF
or PUFF, TRAMPLE or TERRIFY,
GLARE or SCARE, ROAR
or HOLLER — or be one bit
BOTHERSOME and
BEASTLY.

Instead,
he picked up an old
lady's dropped shopping
bag and then watched
some birds.

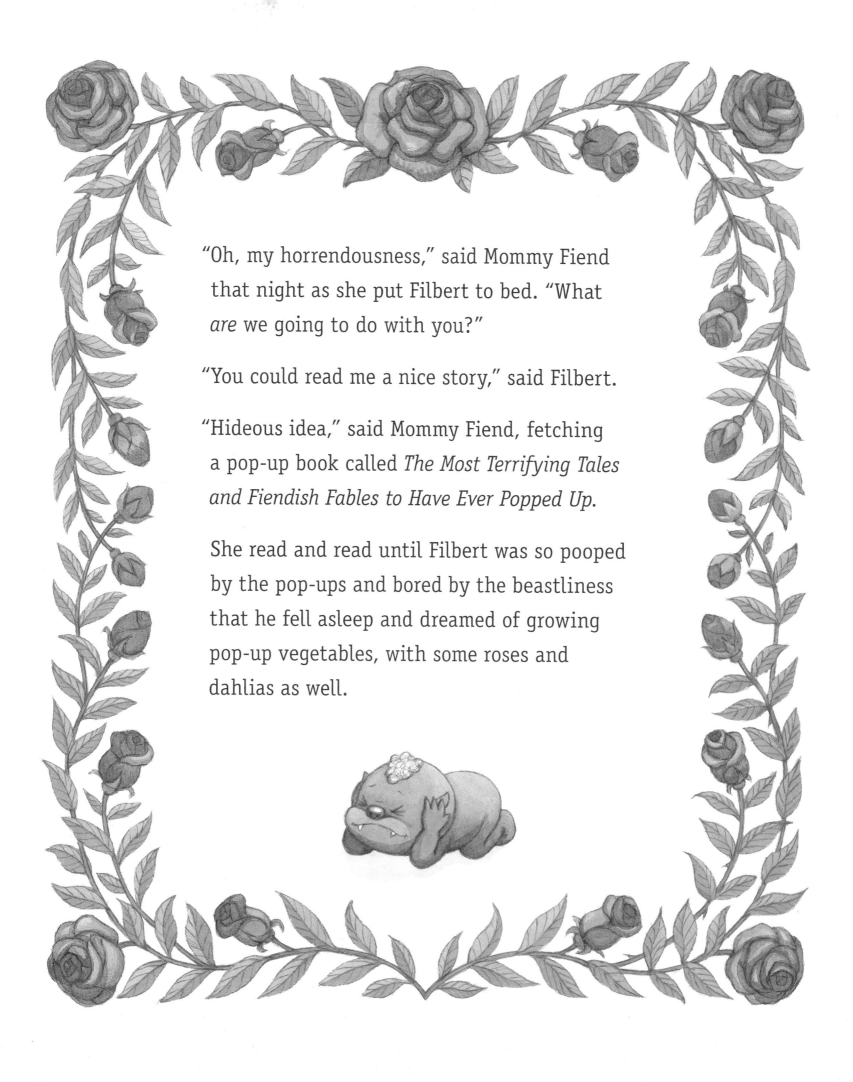

"Oh, my horrendousness," said Mommy Fiend that night as she put Filbert to bed. "What *are* we going to do with you?"

"You could read me a nice story," said Filbert.

"Hideous idea," said Mommy Fiend, fetching a pop-up book called *The Most Terrifying Tales and Fiendish Fables to Have Ever Popped Up.*

She read and read until Filbert was so pooped by the pop-ups and bored by the beastliness that he fell asleep and dreamed of growing pop-up vegetables, with some roses and dahlias as well.

The next day, as it happened,
was the very day Filbert was to start
school. Mommy and Daddy Fiend dropped
him off, saying, "Now, be a proper little
fiend for us. *Promise* you will?"

But Filbert didn't even nod.

He listened to Miss Fearsome-Frizz, his teacher, when she said, "Get ready for Musical Thumps!" and "Everyone on the mat for shriek-and-show, and after that we'll have a purple-paint fight!"

But Filbert didn't join in.

Instead, he built an airplane out of drinking straws. He played cat's cradle in a corner — very quietly — and he hid in the little fiends' bathroom during the entire purple-paint fight.

When he came back, Miss Fearsome-Frizz looked at him suspiciously. "Filbert! You've been *keeping out of the fight,* haven't you?"

"Yes," said Filbert, who never lied because he didn't see the need to.

"Well, I *can't* have such good behavior in my class," Miss Fearsome-Frizz sizzled. "You will go and sit outside on the grassy Good Spot until you've decided to behave like a *proper* little fiend."

So Filbert put on his coat, his horns, and his mittens and ran outside to the grassy Good Spot, where he watched the clouds drifting by and the flowers nodding in the breeze.

Then suddenly, out of nowhere,
came a little angel, flying so fast and furiously that
she wasn't looking where she was going and . . .

BUMP!

She bumped into
the tree and landed in
a heap beside Filbert.

"Hello," said Filbert. "I'm Filbert."

"Hello," said the little angel heap. "I'm Florinda.
 I've been sent out from Angel School for *not* being good enough.
 And I'm *very* furious about it."

"And I've been sent out from Fiend School for being *too* good,"
 said Filbert. "And I'm thinking about it."

"Well, I wish you'd think of a good way to make
 them happy with us *just as we are*!"
 wailed Florinda.

"Hmm . . ."
 said Filbert, jumping up.
"I think I have.
 Here we go!"

Then Filbert took off
his fiery red coat,
his horrifying horns,
and his monstrous mittens
and lent them to Florinda.

Florinda took off
her soft silvery cloak,
her fluffy white wings,
and her golden halo
and lent them to Filbert.

So when Florinda walked into Angel School looking like
a fierce little fiend, everyone *begged* her to get back to
being a not-quite-perfect little angel.

And when Filbert walked into Fiend School looking like
a sweet little angel, everyone *begged* him to get back
to being a not-so-fearsome little fiend.

After that, the angels in Angel School sighed and accepted that Florinda wasn't always as good as angels were expected to be.

And Miss Fearsome-Frizz kept her hair on when Filbert behaved nicely. "At least he's no angel!" she muttered to herself.

And Filbert's daddy and mommy let him be himself without complaining. (Though they did have another baby fiend rather quickly in the hope that he or she would be truly gruesome and ghastly . . . and it has to be said that they were not disappointed.)

As for Filbert and Florinda,
well . . . you can guess what happened to them.
They became best friends.
Why? You know why.

Because together, they were just about
AS GOOD AS IT GETS . . .

a not-quite-perfect little angel
and an almost *always* good little fiend!